KT-477-000

Let the snog fest begin!

This book has been specially compiled and published for World Book Day 2007.

World Book Day is a worldwide celebration of books and reading. This year marks the tenth anniversary of World Book Day in the United Kingdom and Ireland.

For further information please see www.worldbookday.com

World Book Day is made possible by generous sponsorship from National Book Tokens, participating publishers, authors and booksellers. Booksellers who accept the £1 Book Token themselves fund the full cost of redeeming it.

'Let the snog fest begin!'

Georgia Nicolson's guide to life and luuurve

Louise Rennison

HarperCollins *Children's Books*

**Find out more about Georgia and join the Ace Gang at
www.georgianicolson.com**

This book contains extracts from Louise Rennison's series
The Confessions of Georgia Nicolson.

First published in Great Britain in paperback by HarperCollins *Children's Books* in 2007
HarperCollins *Children's Books* is a division of HarperCollins*Publishers* Ltd,
77-85 Fulham Palace Road, Hammersmith, London W6 8JB

www.harpercollinschildrensbooks.co.uk

1

ISBN-13 978-0-00-724404-1
ISBN-10 0-00-724404-5

Printed and bound in Great Britain by
Bookmarque Ltd, Croydon, Surrey

Contents

A Note from Georgia

Bonsoir little chums and chumettes,

My life could be called a triumph, darling, a triumph romance-wise. It could be called that, but actually I have all too often been on the rack of love, and now and again in the oven of despair. So through deep luuurve for you all (and I know I don't know you all personally, but I still love you, just accept it, feel the love and get on with it) I want to help you avoid the snogging disasters that have plagued my life. The little pitfalls that I have tumbled into like a tumbling into thing on a tumbling holiday in Tumble Land. So this helpful little work of geniosity is made up of bits from my vair vair famous and good diaries, that will help you in your professional snogging capacity.

The very first boy fiasco I tried my snogging skills on was Mark Big Gob, who lives up the street from me. When I say Mark Big Gob, that is what I mean - snogging him was a bit like snogging a dolphin. Not that I have. Look, just leave it.

Then there was Whelk Boy, who I actually went to for snogging lessons. He taught me how to avoid bobbing around like a pigeon, trying to decide which side to put my head on in a first snogging encounter.

Things really looked up snogwise when I met Robbie, a.k.a. the SEX GOD. Robbie was the lead singer in The Stiff Dylans and dreamy beyond dreaminess. However, after I had the General and Cosmic and Particular Horns for him (see glossary under "Hoooooorn"), he decided I was too young and went off to Kiwi-a-gogo land.

In the middle of my heartbreakosity, when I was all on my owney in the bakery of pain, along came Masimo, the Italian Stallion, a.k.a. the LUUURVE GOD. And he introduced me to continental type snogging e.g. full-frontal with an Italian accent.

♡ 7

For those of you just TOOO BUSY with your own lives to have bothered to read my diaries (I have written seven of these. Keep up!!! I'm not displaying my all for nothing, you know?) Anyway, for you BUSY people I should explain that the Ace Gang mentioned is my gang of mates at Stalag 14 (school), consisting of:

- the very nearly quite sane (me),

- the slightly bonkers, (Jools and Ellen and Mabs),

- the severely fringed and annoying (Jas)

- and the truly barking mad (Rosie).

Honorary members of the gang are Dave the Laugh, who for a bloke is very nearly human (and also incidentally a top boy at snogging) and Sven, Rosie's boyfriend who comes from... well, actually no one knows where he comes from. It might be Lapland. Wherever he comes from it is a) not England and b) not normal.

Anyway, that is enough rambling in anyone's

language, so let's shut up, pucker up and LET THE SNOG FEST BEGIN!

Georgia
XXX

p.s. There are a variety of loons who appear in my diaries. My parents, Mutti and Vati, are two of the major ones. As is my poo-obsessed little sister Libby. Then there is my grandvati, who regularly sets fire to himself with his pipe, Mr and Mrs Next Door, and my cat Angus, half Scottish wildcat, half tabby domestic, who is as big as a Labrador, only mad. Oh, and there is Uncle Eddie, one of my vati's vair vair sad mates, who is so bald that he looks like a boiled egg in a tracksuit.

You have been warned.

p.p.s. For the quite dim amongst you, and I say that in a caring way, I have divided things up into easy to eat sections.

How not to be a prat and a fool beauty-wise

This section is all to do with preparation for snogging. You can't just wander willy nilly and akimbo into the snogging arena. You have to cleanse and tone to within an inch of your life. And above all else pluck for England and make sure that the orang-utan gene does not make an unwelcome appearance. Hairs shooting out of your crevices are not attractive. However, there are limits...

Never accidentally shave off your eyebrows (unless you like looking like a Klingon)

Thursday August 27th
11:00 a.m.

I've started worrying about what to wear for the first day back at school. It's only eleven days away now. I wonder how much "natural" make-up I can get away with? Concealer is OK – I wonder about mascara. Maybe I should just dye my eyelashes? I hate my eyebrows. I say eyebrows, but in fact it's just the one eyebrow right along my forehead. I may have to do some radical plucking if I can find Mum's tweezers. She hides things from me now because she says that I never replace anything. I'll have to rummage around in her bedroom.

2:00 p.m.

Found the tweezers eventually. Why Mum would think I wouldn't find them in Dad's tie drawer I really don't know. I did find something very strange in the tie drawer as well as the tweezers. It was a sort of apron thing in a special box. I hope against hope that my dad is not a transvestite. It would be more than flesh and blood could stand if I had to "understand" his feminine side. And me and Mum and Libby have to watch while he clatters around in one of Mum's nighties and fluffy mules... We'll probably have to start calling him Daphne.

God, it's painful plucking. I'll have to have a little lie down. The pain is awful, it's made my eyes water like mad.

2:30 p.m.

I can't bear this. I've only taken about five hairs out and my eyes are swollen to twice their normal size.

4:00 p.m.

Cracked it. I'll use Dad's razor.

4:05 p.m.

Sharper than I thought. It's taken off a lot of hair just on one stroke. I'll have to even up the other one.

4:16 p.m.

Bugger it. It looks all right, I think, but I look very surprised in one eye. I'll have to even up the other one now.

6:00 p.m.

Mum nearly dropped Libby when she saw me. Her exact words were, "What in the name of God have you done to yourself, you stupid girl?"

God I hate parents! Me stupid?? They're so stupid. She wishes I was still Libby's age so she could dress me in ridiculous hats with earflaps and ducks on. God, God, God!!!

7:00 p.m.
When Dad came in I could hear them talking about me.

"Mumble mumble... she looks like... mumble mumble," from Mum, then I heard Dad, "She WHAT??? Well... mumble... mumble... grumble..." Stamp, stamp, bang, bang on the door.

"Georgia, what have you done now?"

I shouted from under the blankets – he couldn't get in because I had put a chest of drawers in front of the door – "At least I'm a real woman!!!"

He said through the door, "What in the name of arse is that supposed to mean?"

Honestly, he can be so crude.

10:00 p.m.
Maybe they'll grow back overnight. How long does it take for eyebrows to grow?

Friday August 28th

11:00 a.m.

Eyebrows haven't grown back.

11:15 a.m.

Jas phoned and wanted to go shopping – there's some new make-up range that looks so natural you can't tell you have got any on.

I said, "Do they do eyebrows?"

She said, "Why? What do you mean? Do you mean false eyelashes?"

I said, "No, I mean eyebrows. You know, the hairy bits above your eyes." Honestly friends can be thick.

"Of course they don't do eyebrows. Everyone's got eyebrows. Why would you need a spare pair?"

I said, "I haven't got any any more. I shaved them off by mistake."

She said, "I'm coming round now. Don't do anything until I get there.

Noon

When I opened the door Jas just looked at me like

I was a Klingon. "You look like a Klingon," she said. She really is a dim friend. It's more like having a dog than a friend, actually.

6:00 p.m.
Jas has gone. Her idea of help was to draw some eyebrows on with eyeliner pencil.

Obviously I have to stay in now for ever.

7:00 p.m.
Dad is annoying me so much. He just comes to the door, looks in and laughs, and then he goes away for a bit. He brought Uncle Eddie upstairs for a look. What am I? A daughter or a fairground attraction? Uncle Eddie said, "Never mind, if they don't grow back you and I can go into showbiz. We can do a double act doing impressions of billiard balls." Oh how I laughed. Not.

✻   ✻   ✻

Boy Entrancers

Boy entrancers may hint at a sophisticosity beyond your years, but not if they get stuck together – then they hint that you should be taken to a loony bin...

Friday April 22nd
1:00 a.m.

I have got everything ready for tomorrow night, even though I want to play it cool and just sort of remind Masimo who I am. I am not going to be throwing myself at him or anything. I am going to play the callous sophisticate.

The callous sophisticate with really groovy false eyelashes, or my boy entrancers, as I call them.

Saturday April 23rd
7:00 p.m.

I don't ever remember being this jelloid before, not even when I had Terminal Horn syndrome for the Sex God. I can hardly move my eyelids for mascara and false eyelashes. I wonder if they look natural? I didn't get the ones with the false diamonds in them. I just got the thick long ones.

Oh, I can't take them off now, it took me about a million years to put the glue on and stick them on. It is not as easy as it sounds on the packet. What I go through for luuurve.

Stiff Dylans gig
8:15 p.m.

In the tarting-up area (loos) we reapplied lip gloss for maximum snoggosity.

Rosie said, "What is your cunning plan, Georgia? Full frontal or glaciosity with just a hint of promise?"

I said, "Deffo glaciosity with a hint of p."

"Is that why you are wearing furry eyelashes?"

I gave her my special cross-eyed Klingon look. "These, Rosie, are not false eyelashes. They are boy entrancers. They hint at a sophisticosity beyond my years."

The Ace Gang went out into the club and I had one last check in the mirror. I practised my "sticky eye" technique. God, I was good – I practically got off with myself.

Out in the club it was really kicking, quite dark and groovy. In fact when I first came out of the tarting-up area, I couldn't see anything for a minute until my peepers got used to the lack of light. I don't think the boy entrancers help.

10:00 p.m.

I hadn't even seen Masimo yet. I can hardly remember what he looks like. Maybe I had imagined he was groovy. I hadn't actually stood right next to him. Perhaps he was a bit of a shortarse, or maybe he had an irritating laugh. Or he had grown a goatee. Or he liked elfs... or—

Then the DJ said, "And now it's time for The... Stiff Dylans!!!"

And they came onstage. Everyone except Masimo. Dom said into his mike above the whooping and clapping, "Cheers, thanks a lot, we're back! And tonight we would like you to go wild for our new lead singer. He's not entirely an English person but someone with a touch of Latin blood – calm down, girls – I give you... Masimo. *Ciao*, Masimo."

And Masimo came onstage. Oh, crumbly knees *extraordinaire*. He is, as I may have mentioned before, the Cosmic Horn personified. The girls at the front were going bananas jumping up and down. (Which is not something I would try, even with my extra-firm nunga-nunga holders.)

I said to Jools, "How very little pridenosity they have got."

The joint was really rocking and we had to dance. It was like being at the sheepdog trials and dancing though because Jas had had an argument with Tom, and she was so paranoid about him getting to her we had to circle round her, dancing. When any one of us wanted to go to the piddly-diddly department, we all had to shuffle and dance off together and then shuffle and dance back to our place.

I was exhausted and managed to have a bit of a breather by the stairs, and it was there that Tom got me. "Did Jas tell you? Does she want to, you know, sort of make up? Can't you make her see?"

"Tom, I have to tell you this: I am Jas's friend and we are officially *ignorez*ing you. You are a mirage to me. I can't even see you actually."

He said, "And nothing would make you help me?"

"*Non*, and also we have taken an oath involving torture."

He just looked at me.

"What if I could help you really casually bump into Masimo?"

"Pardon?"

"I met him the other night at snooker."

"You met him... he met you... you he... "

"Yes. And he will come and say hello to me in the break and I could be casually talking to you."

I said with all the dignosity I could, given that my skirt was so tight, "And you think that I would betray my bestest pal Jas just for some bloke I hardly know? When I have taken a solemn vow with Chinese burns and everything?"

Tom looked at me. "If you don't mind me saying so, you are quite literally criminally insane."

The band had left the stage by the time I went back over to Tom. I said to him, "Mission accomplished. She will talk to you, but I have to go over and try to persuade her, but you will know that we are acting."

Tom gave me a hug. As he was hugging me Masimo came from the dressing room. As he walked through the crowd it sort of parted before him. There was an awful lot of flicking of hair and smiling going on. And that was just the boys!!! No, really it was the girls, especially that trollopy Sharon Davies. She's had blonde streaks put in her hair. I don't think they look very natural. Not like my boy entrancers. I put an extra slurp of glue on them when I was in the loo just now so there is no chance of them coming off. I was just watching Masimo. Not directly. I was looking over Tom's shoulder. As I was being Miss Cool I saw Wet Lindsay walk in with her sad mates. She had a ludicrously short skirt on. If I had legs as thin as hers I would wear big inflatable trousers so that I didn't startle anyone. But she is too selfish to bother.

Ohmygiddygod, Masimo was coming our way.

Tom winked at me. Then he called over to Masimo, "Hey, Masimo, *ciao*."

Masimo heard him and smiled and came over. Oh, please please don't let me go to the piddly-diddly department in the middle of the dance floor. When he reached us I could feel the heat of him being near me. Good grief and jelloid knickers akimbo. He said, "Hey, Tom, *ciao* – and it's you. Let me see... the lovely Ginger."

I went, "Hahahahahahahahahahaha" until Tom hit me on the back.

Tom said, "No, this is Georgia. Georgia went out with Robbie for a bit before he went to Whakatane."

Masimo looked me right in the eyes. "Robbie is, how you say in English, not in his right brains to leave you behind." And he smiled again. Phwoar! I had to look down because I couldn't trust myself not to leap on him. I looked down and then I was intending to look up and do that looking up and looking away thing, and also possibly a bit of flicky hair. Unfortunately when I tried to look up again, I couldn't because my boy entrancers had stuck to my bottom lashes. So my eyes stayed shut. They were glued together. I kept trying to open my eyes but I couldn't. In sheer desperadoes I said, "Oh, I love this one." And started wobbling my head around to the music.

The tune was Rolf Harris's "Two Little Boys", the naffest record known to humanity.

Ohmygiddygod what should I do? I kept up the head waggling and I was raising my eyebrows up and down to pull my eyelashes apart. I bet that looked attractive. I thought I'd better do some humming. I started humming along to the tune.

Masimo said, "Would you like to have a drink?"

"Hummmmmmm hummmmmmmm... No thanks, *non grazie*, I must groove to this one."

I must get away. I turned and head-wobbled off. I couldn't see a thing, obviously, so to stop myself from crashing into anything I put my hands out in front of me, but then I thought that would look odd so I tried to fit it into my dancing. I put one hand out in front and waved the other above my head like disco dancing. I knew the loos were sort of to my right and if I could just get there I could rip my boy entrancers off.

My "grooving" arm banged into something soft

and someone said, "Oy, mind my basoomas, you cream-faced loon!"

It was Rosie, thank God. I said to her, "Rosie, lead me to the loos."

She said, "Clear off, you lezzie."

I was still madly flinging my arms around. Hopefully Masimo would think it was the eccentric English way of having a good time. Either that or he would be phoning for the emergency services.

I said to Rosie, "My boy entrancers have stuck together. I can't open my eyes. Do something."

She said, "Quick, put your hands on my shoulders and we'll conga dance over to the loos."

"Rosie, I don't think that's a very good—"

Before I knew it, she had forced my hands on to her shoulders and we were doing the conga. Fifty-five million years later I broke free from the conga line – once we had started doing it, the whole club had joined in. I yelled at Rosie to stop and take me to the loos, but she was having too much of a laugh. I got my hand to my eyes and tried to pry the lashes apart, and that's when it fell off in my hand – the boy entrancer I mean, not my eye.

* * *

Do not go to parties dressed as a stuffed olive (I did, and put it this way I was a snog-free zone)

You know when you are with your girl mates and you think of something really really funny. You know, so funny that you have a laughing attack and can't stop, and you know that you really really should stop because someone is going to kill you if you don't stop laughing. But you still can't stop. Well, whatever it is that you think is so funny – never, ever do that thing in front of boys. Honestly, I mean it. It may seem funny in your room, but then try getting out of your room. Here is my little tale. (I don't mean I have got a little tail and I have spelled it wrong, I just mean... oh, you know what I mean. I am vair vair tired.)

Sunday August 23rd
4:00 p.m.
I blame Jas entirely. It may have been my idea to go as a stuffed olive but she didn't stop me like a pal should do. In fact, she encouraged me. We made

the stuffed olive costume out of chicken wire and green crêpe paper – that was for the "olive" bit. It had little shoulder straps to keep it up and I wore a green T-shirt and green tights underneath. It was the "stuffed" bit that Jas helped with mostly. As I recall, it was she that suggested I use crazy colour to dye my hair and head and face and neck red... like a sort of pimento. It was, I have to say, quite funny at the time. Well, when we were in my room. The difficulty came when I tried to get out of my room. I had to go down the stairs sideways.

When I did get to the door I had to go back and change my tights because my cat Angus had one of his "Call of the Wilds" episodes.

He really is completely bonkers. We got him when we went on holiday to Loch Lomond. On the last day I found him wandering around the garden of the guest-house we were staying in. Tarry-a-Wee-While, it was called. That should give you some idea of what the holiday was like.

I should have guessed all was not entirely well in the cat department when I picked him up and he began savaging my cardigan. But he was such a lovely looking kitten, all tabby and long-haired, with huge yellow eyes. Even as a kitten he looked like a small dog. I begged and pleaded to take him home.

"He'll die here, he has no mummy or daddy," I said plaintively.

My dad said, "He's probably eaten them." Honestly, he can be callous. I worked on Mum and in the end I brought him home. The Scottish landlady did say she thought he was probably mixed breed, half domestic tabby and half Scottish wildcat. I remember thinking, *Oh, that will be exotic.* I didn't realise that he would grow to the size of a small Labrador, only mad. I used to drag him around on a lead but, as I explained to Mrs Next Door, he ate it.

Anyway, sometimes he hears the call of the Scottish highlands. So, as I was passing by as a stuffed olive he leaped out from his concealed hiding-place behind the curtains (or his lair, as I suppose he imagined it in his cat brain) and attacked my tights or "prey". I couldn't break his hold by banging his head because he was darting from side to side. In the end I managed to reach the outdoor brush by the door and beat him off with it.

Then I couldn't get in Dad's Volvo. Dad said, "Why don't you take off the olive bit and we'll stick it in the boot."

Honestly, what is the point? I said, "Dad, if you think I am sitting next to you in a green T-shirt and tights, you're mad."

He got all shirty like parents do as soon as you point out how stupid and useless they are. "Well, you'll have to walk, then... I'll drive along really slowly with Jas and you walk alongside."

I couldn't believe it. "If I have to walk, why don't Jas and I both walk there and forget about the car?"

He got that stupid, tight-lipped look that dads get when they think they are being reasonable. "Because I want to be sure of where you are going. I don't want you out wandering the streets at night."

Unbelievable! I said, "What would I be doing walking the streets at night as a stuffed olive...

gatecrashing cocktail parties?"

Jas smirked but Dad got all outraged parenty. "Don't you speak to me like that, otherwise you won't go out at all."

What is the point?

When we did eventually get to the party (me walking next to Dad's Volvo driving at five miles an hour), I had a horrible time. Everyone laughed at first but then more or less ignored me. In a mood of defiant stuffed oliveness I did have a dance by myself but things kept crashing to the floor around me. The host asked me if I would sit down. I had a go at that but it was useless. In the end I was at the gate for about an hour before Dad arrived, and I did stick the olive bit in the boot. We didn't speak on the way home.

Jas, on the other hand, had a great time. She said she was surrounded by Tarzans and Robin Hoods and James Bonds. (Boys have very vivid imaginations... not.)

I was feeling a bit moody as we did the "recall" bit. I said bitterly, "Well, I could have been surrounded by boys if I hadn't been dressed as an olive."

Jas said, "Georgia, you thought it was funny and I thought it was funny but you have to remember that boys don't think girls are for funniness."

She looked annoyingly "wise" and "mature". What the hell did she know about boys? God, she had an annoying fringe. Shut up, fringey.

I said, "Oh yeah, so that's what they want, is it? Boys? They want simpering girly-wirlys in catsuits?"

Through my bedroom window I could see next door's poodle leaping up and down at our fence, yapping. It would be trying to scare off our cat Angus... fat chance.

Jas was going on and on wisely. "Yes they do, I think they do like girls who are a bit soft and not so, well... you know."

She was zipping up her rucksack. I looked at her. "Not so what?" I asked.

She said, "I have to go, we have an early supper."

As she left my room I knew I should shut up. But you know when you should shut up because you really should just shut up... but you keep on and on anyway? Well, I had that.

"Go on... not so what?" I insisted.

She mumbled something as she went down the stairs.

I yelled at her as she went through the door, "Not so like me you mean, don't you?!!!"

11:00 p.m.

I can already feel myself getting fed up with boys and I haven't had anything to do with them yet.

Midnight

Oh God, please, please don't make me have to be a lesbian like Hairy Kate or Miss Stamp.

* * *

Always wear a sturdy over-the-shoulder-boulder-holder

Never, even on a sunny windless day, allow your nunga-nungas the freedom to live free and wild. There could be nasty accidents snogging-wise.

Tuesday July 27th
SG Day
Setting off to his house
7:00 p.m.
It's taken most of the day to achieve my natural make-up look. Just a subtle touch to enhance my natural beauty. I wanted the just-tumbled-out-of-bed look, so I only used undercover concealer, foundation, hint of bronzer, eye pencil, eight layers of mascara, lip liner, lippy and lip gloss, and I left it at that.

7:20 p.m.
Jas phoned to wish me luck. She said, "Tell me all about it when you get home. Remember what number you get up to on the snogging scale. Are you

♡ 33

wearing a bra? I think it would be wise because you don't want to wobble all over the place."

I said, "Goodbye, Jas."

I'm not wearing a bra; I thought I would go free and akimbo. I just won't make any sudden movements.

Walking down Arundel Street
7:30 p.m.

Brrr, not quite as warm and bright as it was earlier. A bit overcast, actually, and... oh no... it's starting to rain! It's too far to go back home for an umby... it will probably stop in a minute.

7:40 p.m.

Outside Robbie's gate. It really is raining quite hard now. I'm wet through and really cold. I think my trousers have shrunk; they are hugging my bottom in a vice-like grip. I wonder if I look all right?

I'll nip into the telephone box opposite his house and check my mirror.

In the telephone box
7:45 p.m.
My trousers have shrunk so tight around my bottom that I can't bend my legs. This is hopeless. Brrr. Why is everything going wrong? I can't go to see the Sex God looking like this. I'll have to phone him up and say I'm ill.

7:50 p.m.
SG answered the phone, "Hello."

Swoon swoon.

I said, "Roggie, nit's ne, Neorgia."

"What's wrong with your voice?"

"Der nl'd gat a trrible cold nd Im nin bed."

"Do they have beds in telephone boxes?"

"Dnno."

"Georgia, I can see you through the window."

When I looked across at his house, he waved at me. Oh GODDDDDD!!!!!!

He said, "Come over."

What can I do, what can I do? My top is all wet. And there are two bumpy things in it. Great! It looks like I've got two peas down the front of my top. Typical, the only thing Mum has ever ironed for me and she has ironed it wrong.

As I walked up to the door I tried to flatten out the bumpy bits. But it wasn't my top sticking up... it was ME!!! My nipples!!!!! What were they doing?!!! Why were they sticking out? I hadn't told them to do that. How could I get them back in again? I'd have to cross my arms in a casual way and hope he didn't offer me a cup of coffee.

*   *   *

Shoefeet

If you have giant feet, like what I have, do not try and squeeze them into little midget shoes. It will all end in tears. And perhaps the local casualty department...

Saturday 4th June
Churchill Square
11:00 a.m.
Rosie said, "In this sort of situation, she who dares shops." So in preparation for the Battle of the Chicks. (Could Masimo really choose stupid stick-insecty, no-foreheady Wet Lindsay over me?) I am going to get a fabby and marvy pair of shoes.

Ravel
11:30 a.m.
I saw these cool shoes in the window, with a bit of a kitten heel and some groovy strappy bits round the toes and the heel.

In the shoe shop

We all trooped in and I asked for my size. The woman said the biggest they had was a size four until next week.

Next week! Is she mad? I have to go the gig, like, tonight!

I said to her, "OK, please bring me them."

Jas said, "What's the point of that, you take a size seven?"

"Sometimes."

Rosie, who was trying on some ludicrous furry boots that made her look like a yeti, said, "So do your feet change size then?"

I said, "Well, you know, it *says* a size seven, but then if they are made in Japan where they have very tiny feet, size seven is like a size fifteen over here."

They all looked at me.

Then the lady with the shoes came back. They were groovy as anything. Masimo would love them because, as every fool knows, Italians are the mistresses of footwear.

Five minutes later

Blimey. I couldn't get my heels in. I said politely to the lady, "Have you got a horn?"

And that set the gang off into hysterics.

She looked at us like we were loons, but went off to get the shoehorn.

Five minutes later

Got them on! Yesss!!

The lady in the shop said, "Are you sure they fit? Walk around in them."

The gang were all slouched about waiting for me not to be able to walk. I got up. Ouch ouch and double *merde* and ouch. They were bloody aggers. I looked in the mirror. They looked fab. I must have them; I must go through the pain for him. I smiled like a loon. "Do you know, it's amazing, they are sooooo comfy as well as being groovy. It's almost like wearing slippers."

Bedroom

1:00 p.m.

I have stuffed my new shoes with newspapers to

try and stretch them.

1:30 p.m.
Mum came snuffling around. "Give us a look at your new shoes."

I said, "Oh, I'll show you later when I'm all dressed up."

In my room
5:45 p.m.
I have two mirrors arranged so that I can see back and front. I am so smoothy everywhere that I am like a human billiard ball – there is not one single lurking rogue hair on my entire body. I am a lurker-free zone, and I have at least got my base coat of make-up on.

7:00 p.m.
Just about ready. I am not going to risk the boy entrancers, even though they are fab and entrance boys like billio. I don't want to take any risks gluewise. I've put eight coats of mascara on, so that should do the trick. I put on one coat and

then put talcum powder over it and then another coat and so on. I can hardly lift my top lids up, but I like to think that gives me a mysterious sexualosity.

7:15 p.m.
My little blue skirt looks vair fab and I have put fake tan on my legs to top up my Hamburger-a-gogo browniness. I don't think you can really see the streaky bits unless you're at floor level, and who is going to be there? Apart from midget lesbians. I have got my strict bra on, the one that takes no nonsense from my basoomas.

7:25 p.m.
Mum called up: "Can I come and see what you're wearing?"

Oh God.

I put my shoes on.

OH my God!!! Ag city Arizona! They were made for a child! I pushed my feet in and managed to get them on. And stood up. If I walked about I would probably get used to them.

Mum came in. "Wow. You look really groovy! Is this for the Italian Stallion?"

Shut up. Please shut up.

Then she noticed my shoes. "Are they your new shoes? They are gorge, aren't they? Aren't they a bit too small for you?"

I said, smiling widely, "Gosh, no, if anything they are a bit slack."

She was still looking at them. "What size are they?"

I looked at my watch and said, "Crikey O'Reilly, is that the time? I promised to meet the gang at seven thirty. S'later."

I dashed off down the stairs. Ouch ouch, aggers aggers. Bugger bugger bum.

On the way to Jas's

My God, these shoes hurt. On the plus side I think they're cutting off the blood supply to my feet, so with a bit of luck my feet will be numb soon. I had to sit up on a wall for a resties just round the corner from Jas's house.

7:45 p.m.

As we walked along Jas said, "Do you want to go to the loo? You're walking funny."

Stiff Dylans gig
9:00 p.m.

Vair vair dark in the club – and rammed. We edged around to the bar; it took a while to get used to the dark. Especially if your eyes were weighed down with one pound of mascara and talcum powder. Some bulky girl trod on my toe as she was going by with her lardy mates. I shouted out, "Bloody hell in a hand basket, ouch ouch! Bollocking bugger bugger bum!!!"

Jas said, "Are you sure your shoes are OK?"

I said, "Jas, some complete imbecile of gigantic proportions has just trodden on my foot. That is why I am leaping like a loon."

I might actually have to slip off for a quick lie down in the loos and put my feet up on the loo seat.

But then "all pain dropped away from my tootsies forsooth", as Billy so eloquently put it in his famous sonnet "Ode to my feet". Masimo came up to the bar. He looked mega-cool (and a half). He doesn't look like English boys. He's more sophis. He was wearing a cool, pale blue Italian suit with a T-shirt. Like me, he was wearing fabby shoes. (Although his didn't have kitten heels and he didn't look like he was going to wet himself.)

I put my shoulders back to give a bit of nunga emphasis (looking round first to make sure I didn't knock anyone over). Also, I let my mouth drop open a bit and put my tongue behind my bottom teeth. Like Britney Spears but without the big tongue piercing.

I was deliberately not acknowledging Masimo. I was absolutely tip-top full of glaciosity.

Jas, Ellen and Mabs were, however, full of stupidosity. They all came crowding round me going, "Have you seen him? Have you seen him? He's at the bar, over there – look, can you see him?" And so on. Soooo annoying and uncool.

I was still doing my tongue behind the teeth thing, so I said, "Thlear off, tho away, thleave me ayown."

I pretended to wave at someone in Masimo's

direction. He caught my eye and smiled. I slightly smiled, and he began to come across to me. Oh, I love him I love him. But no! Remember the plan. I smiled again and then I forced myself to walk away. And not look back. Cor, how difficult was this? But I must do it. I must keep up my glaciosity.

9:30 p.m.
No sign of my rival in love, the incredibly useless stick insect of the universe and back. Good. Oh, maybe she's dead. How sad. Never mind.

The Stiff Dylans are coming on in a minute.

9:40 p.m.
Wow, the place has gone hog wild!!! Girls were shrieking when Masimo came to the microphone and said, "*Ciao*. We are back."

10:15 p.m.
I am quite literally in a dance inferno. Hit it, lads! The whole club is kicking. All the boys are fit and cool and Masimo is a brilliant singer and sooooo sexy on stage.

10:40 p.m.

I'm sweating a bit so I had better go and cool myself down in the loos; the last thing a Luuurve God wants is a slippery girlfriend. I have been doing some of my best moves in front of him. Just subtly, you know, nothing flash, although I did have to shove Jas quite hard once or twice to get her to let me in. Wet Lindsay turned up and has been dancing in front of him with her eyes fixed on him like she was trying to hypnotise him.

I said to Ro Ro, "As the Swan of Avon said in his famous snogging comedy *Midsummer Night's Snog*, when you wanteth to snog a Luuurve God, do not prithee danceth about like a prat with stick-insect legs."

Rosie said, "Ye are wiseth in the extremeth, my palleth. Billy also saideth, 'Forsooth and lack a day, do not have ye a tiny forehead, otherwise you are simply askething for a duffing-up scenario...eth'."

Then we laughed like the proverbial draineth.

In the tarts' enclosure

Blimey! Good job I did a make-up check; I looked like a red-faced loon.

I must take my shoes off for a moment. I went into a piddly-diddly kiosk and sat down on the loo seat. Hmmm, my feet looked a bit red and swollen; maybe I should take my shoes off. But if I got them off I might never get them back on. I got down on the floor and put my feet up. Ohhh, that was a bit better. I lay there for a moment feeling a bit miz, but then I remembered that I was not a facsimile of a sham. I was following my dream, I was living the dream! I struggled up to my feet. Owwww... *Sacré* bloody *bleu*.

Back in the club

The band were having a break – no sign of them. I could see Wet Lindsay hovering around near the dressing-room door. Appalling tart. The Ace Gang were all off grooving. Rosie shouted over, "Come and dance, we're having a groovathon."

I said, "I think I'll sit this one out and just, you know, absorb the vibes."

Rosie said, "You mean your feet are hurting because you are wearing baby's shoes."

I gave her my cross-eyed Klingon look and she nutcased off.

Sitting down, I was doing a bit of shoulder dancing to the music when an arm appeared in front of me and handed me a drink. It was a brown arm, it had a gold ring on the third finger. I looked up, and it was Masimo's arm. And he was attached to it.

He smiled down at me. "*Ciao*, you are having tired from dancing?"

I went red – thank God it was dark. I took a big gulp from the drink and practically choked myself, but I managed to say, "Yes, I mean, *sí*. I am indeed having a tired from dancing, yes indeedy."

He said, "It is long since I have seen you. I am glad you came. I would like, if you would like, to have your telephone number."

Oh now, what was the right response to that? Glaciosity requires that I say something like, "Maybe some other time." But he is a Luuurve God. He is bending over me, his gorgey lips are only inches away from mine.

Anyway, I was saved the trouble of doing anything because Dom came over. "Hi, Georgia, long time no dig. How are you?"

Before I could say anything he went on to Masimo. "Listen, mate, sorry to drag you away, but some bloke wants to talk to us about a tour in the North. Can you come over?"

Masimo looked at me with those amazing amber eyes. "I will see you later."

And he touched my shoulder and squeezed it very gently.

Hobbled over to the groovathon and bobbed around trying to talk to Rosie as Sven flung her about like a deflated balloon.

Pant pant, groove groove. "He's asked me for my phone number!"

Rosie yelled, "Result! Or Resultio, as we must say!"

11:30 p.m.
Band back on.

I am sooo excited. I said to Jas, "Do you think I should accidentally hang around as he comes off stage at the next break?"

Jas said, "I would hang around. I mean, it's ridiculous playing silly games, isn't it?"

Rosie said, "Yes, I think cut to the action – go up and give him the phone number and then leave."

Hmmmm. Yes, that sounded good. I lurked at the back of the club near the tarts' wardrobes for a moment to sit down on the stairs. My tootsies were soooooo sore. I tried to ease my feet in my shoes but they wouldn't move. I must save my tootsies for a last walk across to give Masimo my telephone number.

12:30 a.m.
Outside the cloakroom getting our coats out. The band must be going to come out soon. I put my coat on slowly.

I was so distracted by my poor throbbing tootsies that at first I didn't sense the Luuurve presence. He was just coming out of the dressing room, putting his jacket on. How come even putting his jacket on was sexy?

I had the Particular and Cosmic Horns and a heavy dose of red-bottomosity.

He turned round to say something to one of the others, and Wet Lindsay appeared like the Bride of Dracula. She just appeared from nowhere. She was playing with her hair and she trailed her hand across Masimo's arm. He looked round and saw her and smiled. She kissed his cheek and said something in his ear. He looked at her and sort of shrugged his shoulders. She smiled and then linked arms with him and they went off together.

Oh God.

1:00 a.m.
And we had to walk all the way home because we had done the usual "Jas's dad is picking us up" to my dad and "Georgia's dad is picking us up" to Jas's. In a fit of desperation I thought about phoning Vati and telling him we were stuck, but then I would have to talk to him, and I didn't want to talk ever again.

Lying quite literally in my bed of pain
2:30 a.m.
I have tried to get my shoes off but I am so tired

and upset I can't be bothered to struggle with them. So I've left them on and put my jimmyjams on over them. My feet hurt like billio, but not as much as my heart.

2:35 a.m.
What is it with boys and Wet Lindsay?

I dither about for hours thinking, *Shall I have glaciosity or shall I have boldnosity? What botty huggers shall I wear? Is the orang-utan gene making a surprise appearance?* and so on, for hours and hours. And she just goes up to him and says, "Come with me," and off he goes.

Unbelievable.

Sunday 5th June
10:00 a.m.
I woke up and I saw my shoefeet looking at me from the bottom of the bed.

Then I felt the pain... but I am going to have to bear it and take them off.

10:15 a.m.

Oh please. My shoes are embedded in my feet. My skin has been cut by the straps and then in the night everything has all swollen up. You can't even see the straps because the flesh has covered them up. Oh brilliant. Now I will have to have my feet cut off.

10:30 a.m.

Worse than that, I am going to have to ask Mum for help because I can't walk.

11:00 a.m.

Mum bustled into my room. When I heard her I put my shoefeet under the blankets. She said, "Come on and have some breakfast. Dad's taken Libbs round to Josh's, so it's just you and me. We can do something nice if you like."

I said, "It will have to be something that doesn't involve walking about."

She said, "Don't tell me you are tired. Honestly, I had so much energy at your age – I'd go to parties and then play tennis the next day."

I had to tell her about the shoes. Then I showed her my feet. She went ballisticisimus. "You STUPID stupid girl. Honestly you have done some stupid stupid things in your time, but this takes the biscuit of stupidity. How could you do this to yourself? I told you about those shoes! Look at your lovely feet – ruined!!!" And so on for about four centuries.

Mum had a go at getting them off herself, but I couldn't bear the pain, and in the end she said, "I'm going to have to phone for the doctor. On a Sunday."

Oh nooooo. I am so humiliated.

1:00 p.m.

I saw Dr Clooney's car arrive in the driveway and he got out. I hobbled back into bed – ouch ouch and double ouch.

Thank goodness Vati was out.

I heard giggling from downstairs.

1:25 p.m.

Oh yes, that's right, Mutti, just chat and flirt with

Dr Clooney while I lie up here with my dancing days over. Honestly.

Eventually Mum and Dr Clooney came up. My mum had changed into her short black dress and done her hair and make-up. Vair vair sad.

Dr Clooney gave me his crinkly smile. "Well, well, this is a first for me."

He is nice though, very reassuring and funny. He didn't ramble on at me. He just looked at my feet and pulled a bit and I went, "Owwwwww."

Then he said, "Hmmm, I'm going to have to give you a local anaesthetic and cut them off."

And I said, "Oh, doctor, can't you save them?"

And he started saying that he meant the shoes, not my feet, and I said, "I know. Can't you save them?"

Mum gave me her worst look, but Dr Clooney thought it was vair *amusant*.

2:00 p.m.

This is quite nice, actually, in a painful way. Dr Clooney cut off the straps and pulled the bits out with tweezers. He even put some stitches in the deep cuts in my feet. It hurt A LOT but I was brave as a bee on army manoeuvres. They are all bandaged up. Mum is bringing me snacks.

She sat down on my bed and I let her, I don't know why, I am probably weak.

She said, "So, Stumpy, did you have a nice time last night at least?"

I blurted out, "Well, it was mega-fab at first because Masimo asked me for my phone number, but then at the end Wet Lindsay made him go home with her."

Mum said, "I used to know a girl like Wet Lindsay. She got married to a boy I really liked."

I said, "Oh thanks, Mum, you're really cheering me up."

And she said, "Well, every cloud has a silver lining, because she is really really unhappily married. So all's well that ends well."

Sometimes my mum, and I don't want to get carried away by this, but sometimes she can be almost like a real person.

* * *

Avoid your "family"

This section is sooo important I can't stress it enough. If you are unfortunately not an orphan and have a mutti, a vati and a little sister who is obsessed with poo – and also an insane cat... oh, and a grandvati who has a girlfriend called Maisie who knits all the time, and is in fact practically knitted herself – well, keep prospective snoggees away from them at all times. That is if you ever want to snog again. That's all I have to say on the matter.

"Georgia did a big poo."

Bum-oley talk from little brothers and sisters...

Saturday September 26th
10:00 a.m.
Went for a moody autumn walk with my little sister Libby in her pushchair. She was singing, "I am the Queen, oh, I am the Queen." She wouldn't take off the fairy wings that I had made for her. It

was a nightmare getting her into the pushchair. The clouds were scudding across the sky but it was quite sunny and crisp. I cheered up enough to join in the singing with Libby. We were both yelling, "I am the Queen, oh, I am the Queen!" and that's when he got out of a red mini. Robbie. The SG. He saw me and said, "Oh hello, we've met before, haven't we?"

I smiled brilliantly, trying to do it without making my nose spread out over all my face. It's a question of relaxing the mouth, putting the tongue behind the back teeth but slightly flaring the nostrils so that they don't go wild. He looked at me a bit oddly.

"Apples," I said wittily.

"Oh yeah," he said, "the shop, you and your friend."

He smiled again. He was dreamy when he smiled. Then he bent down to Libby who, true to form, gave him one of her scary "I am a crazy child" looks. She said, "I am the queen," and he said, "Are you?" (Ooohhh, he's so lovely to children.)

Then Libby said, "Yes, I am the queen and Georgia did a big poo this morning."

I couldn't believe it. He could not believe it. Nobody could believe it. It was unbelievable, that's why. He stood up quickly and I said, "Er, well, I'd better be going."

And he said, "Yes, see you later."

And I thought, Think Sharon Stone, think Sharon Stone. So I said, "Yes, well I'll probably see you at Katie's party."

And he said, "No, I'm not going, I'm doing something else that night."

7:00 p.m.
"Georgia did a big poo..."

7:05 p.m.
"No, I'm not going, I'm doing something else that night."

7:06 p.m.
Does life get any worse?

* * *

"Botty Boy!"

Yet more bum-oley talk...

Saturday April 16th
8:25 p.m.

Oh *quelle dommage*, Gordy, Angus and Naomi's unnatural and googley eyed offspring is wrestling with his own tail and the tail is winning, so Libby has turned her attention to me. Oh dear.

"Gingey, let's go play outside now."

"Darling, it's nearly bedtime. I know... we could read *Heidi*."

That's when the *Heidi* book hit me quite hard on the head. Libby had apparently gone off cheese and lederhosen. She was stamping her little foot.

"Outside, naughty boy... OUTSIDE!"

Oh hell's biscuits.

And she wouldn't even get dressed. I had to put a blanket over her jimmyjams (at least she had the bottoms on, for once). She was leaping around, yelling "Hickory dickory dot, the cow leapt over the SPOOOOON!!"

I opened the front door and she went leaping out into the dark night. Angus looked down at us from the wall and casually biffed me with his paw. Thanks for your help, furry pal. When we got to the gate I said to Libbs, "There, that was nice leaping, wasn't it? Let's go back to snuggly buggly bed and—"

But she had undone the gate and was leaping away down the street in her blanket. I went after her and tried to pick her up. She nearly had my eye out.

Ten minutes later we were still leaping "over the spoon". My plan was to leap with her and sort of round her up and head her back to our house. But I'd just get her in the right direction and she would do some quick leaps and get round me again. By this stage we had got halfway down Baron's Street, and when I looked up from another failed attempt to head Libby off I saw Dom from The Stiff Dylans getting out of his van with his guitar. Probably turning up for a jamming session at the Phoenix. Libby was leaping in a circle, so I had a chance to smile at Dom.

He said, "Hey, hi, how are you, Georgia? And Libby..."

Libby ignored him because she was busy leaping. But she still managed to tell him, "Gordon pooed in the bath."

Dom said, "I won't even ask. Have you heard from Robbie?"

I felt a bit tearful. "Yeah, he really likes it in New Zealand."

Dom said, "Yeah. I heard. Pity. Ah well... erm, come to the gig on the eighth. We've re-formed and got a cool new singer, so it looks like the record deal might go ahead."

I said, "You've got a new singer, yes, well, that's cool... "

I was thinking, *Yes, that is cool if you can replace a Sex God, which you can't, even if he is a bit obsessed with vegetables.* But I didn't say that.

A silver scooter tore round the corner and stopped outside the Phoenix.

Dom said, "This is him actually, Masimo."

So, at last, this was the so-called Italian-American pseudo Sex God. Huh. How interested was I out of ten? Minus twelve. Unfortunately Libby was interested in the noise of the scooter, and also because it had mirrors and stuff on it. She went leaping over to the scooter.

I yelled, "Libby, come back here now!"

One word from me and she does as she likes. I could hear her saying to the new singer, who was bending over taking off his helmet, "Heggo, I am a moo cow."

Oh bloody Blimey O'Reilly.

I went and got hold of her round the arms, pinning them down so that she couldn't hit me, and lifted her up. But with an alarming change of mood she started kissing me really wildy all over my hair and face. She was ruffling my hair up and messing up my lip gloss. Very very annoying and wet.

"I LOBE you, my Ginger."

I hadn't actually looked at the pretend Sex God as I was busy trying to wrestle with Libby, but then he spoke with an accent that was quite Italian.

"Hello, Ginger. And *ciao*, little moo cow."

I looked at him. Ohmygiddygodstrousers. He

was absolutely gorgeous. Really really gorgey. Really gorgey! And I do mean gorgey. That's why I said it. He had very black wavy hair and a tan – a tan in England in April. And he had eyes and teeth and a mouth. He had a back, front, sides, arms, everything. His mouth wasn't as big as Mark Big Gob's (whose was?) but it was on the generous side. And he had really long eyelashes and AMBER eyes. In fact he had eyes like someone I knew, and then I realised he had eyes like Angus. How freaky deaky!! They were the same colour as Angus's! But they didn't have that casual madnosity that Angus's had. In fact they were smiley and soft and dreamy.

Then I realised that about two hundred years had passed since he had said hello.

I forced Libby's mouth off the back of my neck (in a loving and caring way). I thought, *Act natural and normal, do not under any circumstances have an uncontrollable laughing attack.* I took a deep breath. "Ah yes well, er ciao to you too. I'm not really ginger, it's just a trick of the light. Hahahahahahaha."

Oh brilliant, I was having an uncontrollable laughing attack.

Dom must have realised that my brain had dropped out because he said, "Masimo, this is Georgia. Georgia, this is Masimo, our new lead singer. Georgia was, erm, friendly with Robbie."

Masimo. Masimo. Whohoa Masimo! I must get a grip. Masimo was locking up his scooter. He looked up and looked me straight in the eye. I managed not to fall over. He said, "Well, Georgia, it was really nice to meet you, I hope we meet again. *Ciao*."

Then they walked off to go into the Phoenix.

I said, "Yes, *ciao*."

And Libby shouted, "Night-night, botty boy!"

I turned round and carried her off as fast as I could.

"Libby, why did you say that naughty thing? Don't say it again!"

Libby was singing, "Have you seen the botty boy, the botty boy, the botty boy... "

Where does she get all this stuff from?

* * *

Il Ministrone

Look, I have already told you to keep your vati under control. Here is what happens if you don't...

Monday 6th June
7:35 p.m.

I heard the roar of an engine. Knowing my life, it would be Grandad on a motorbike in a leather all-in-one suit. And Maisie on the back in a knitted bikini.

I peeped out of my window – and practically fell out of it.

It was Masimo!!! Honestly. On his scooter. He was under my window and just switching the engine off.

I must run, run like the wind to... oh no, not since the shoefeet incident. I must hobble, hobble like the wind to... no, no, what I must do is – I must remain calm. Calm calm. While all around you everyone is losing their minds you must, you must... put some bloody make-up on immediately, you complete arse!!

Scrabble, scrabble, mascara... lippy and gloss... eyeshadow... please please don't do shaky hand now – I don't want to be a panda with huge feet!!!

Fluffy hair fluffy hair...

What was going on now? What? What???

Mid mascara, did a hobble-trot to the window and looked out.

There was just his scooter there. Like the Vespa Celeste. Had Angus eaten him?

Then I heard the doorbell ring.

Ohgoddygod.

Put something on. Disguise the feet!

Easier said than done.

I must have something.

Scrabbled through my wardrobe.

What about my extra-long jeans? Yes, yes, good thinking. Extra-long jeans, bit of a crouchy leg and... I looked in the full-length mirror. Yes, yes, that would do, you couldn't see my feet at all. I must remember to crouch, though, and not hobble.

Right, right, I am ready for when Dad starts his

ludicrous shouting up the stairs. It's OK though, because he will just say tummy bug, not shoes cut off.

I must not mention shoes cut off. No one should.

Good, good, that is good.

Excellent.

7:40 p.m.
What was going on? Couldn't they understand what Masimo was saying? His English wasn't that bad.

8:00 p.m.
What was going on? Surely Masimo hadn't come round to see my mum and dad, had he? With my life, I wouldn't be surprised by anything. Perhaps like Dave the Laugh, Masimo fancies my mum.

I crept and shuffled to the top of the stairs. They were in the living room, so I could just hear the muffled sound of voices. Then Libby came bustling along the hall and opened the door to the front room. She waddled into the lounge, saying,

"Gordy has done a big poo in his din dins."

Dear Lord.

8:10 p.m.

I had to rush back into my bedroom because Mum suddenly came out of the room to the kitchen and shouted up to me, "Georgia, I know you are at the top of the stairs. Come down – you have a visitor and your father wants to speak to you."

My father?

Wants to speak to me?

I have a visitor?

It's like *Blithering Heights*. If Masimo is dressed in tight breeches and a cravat, I will truly go mad.

I felt really really sick.

I went into the kitchen first. Mum was making filter coffee. Blimey. I said to her, "What is going on?"

She said, "Oh, we were just having a chat with Masimo. He's lovely, isn't he?"

"Having a chat? Having a CHAT? You have left Vati having a CHAT with someone I never ever want him to talk to about anything. Having a chat about what?"

"Well, he has come to ask us, and in particular your father, if it is all right for him to take you out to dinner next week."

I was quite literally speechless.

8:15 p.m.

Mum made me go into the front room.

Masimo was sitting on the sofa with Libby on his knee. He stood up with her in his arms when I walked in and then he smiled. And when he did that my heart sang. Despite the fresh hell that was about to occur, he was sooooo gorgey.

Vati was standing up in front of the fireplace with his hands behind his back. Then I realised he was smoking a cigar. He never smoked cigars except at Christmas, and then he was sick. What the hell was going on?

He said, "Ah, hello, Georgia. Masimo and I have just been having a chat."

Oh dear God he was using that word again.

Masimo said, "*Ciao*, Georgia."

My vati said, "Do sit down, Georgia. Connie."

It was like being in a cross between a horror film and *My Fair Lady*.

I didn't know what else to do, so I sat down and so did Mum. As soon as we did, Vati and Masimo sat down as well. I fought an overwhelming desire to stand up again to see if they would stand up too.

Dad said, "Masimo has come round to ask if it is all right for him to take you out, and I think after careful thought and a few ground rules that... it would be... acceptable to your mother and myself."

Has he really snapped? He works for the Waterboard, drowning people and driving them out of their homes, but he is not in the Mafia.

He went rambling on about curfews and behaviour. Like the Godfather. He will probably expect us to call him Il Ministrone. Complete and utter bollocks. About honour and his family reputation and so on. I was so so embarrassed. And Masimo just said stuff like, "Of course, I will, how you say, take *molto – mi dispiace*, I am sorry for my English, I will take great care of your daughter."

He smiled at me. "She will even have her own helmet."

And Mum laughed like a crazy person, like "helmet" was the funniest word she had ever heard.

9:00 p.m.
I only got a chance to speak to Masimo right at the end of the nightmare scenario. When he went out to go off on his bike I went out to the gate with him. I said, "Masimo, I am so sorry about my parents. I am *dispiaggio* times a million about them."

He smiled and said, "I thought it was the only way I will get your attention. Now I have your attention, no?"

"Oh yes, you have sure as sure as... eggs... have my attention, matey."

He laughed. "I like it when you speak, it is like..."

"Rubbish?"

He laughed again and handed me a piece of paper. "Here, this is for you. Phone me, *caro*, and let me know if you still would like to see me on Tuesday. *Ciao*."

He looked at me with that unwavering look he has. Oh dear God, I had crumbly knees and jelloid knickers and I sooo wanted to go to the piddly-diddly department.

Then he roared off.

9:05 p.m.

Went back into the house. With a bit of luck I could get in without being seen by the seeing-eye dogs. But oh no, no such luck. Vati came out of the front room. "He seems like a nice young chap. Keen on sports and so on. Good family, healthy lifestyle."

I said, "Shiny nose, glossy coat, that sort of thing."

He said, "I said to your mum that you're not old enough for boys, you should be concentrating on your studies."

Oh, blimey, I had wandered into the twilight world of Daddom. I wandered off as quickly as I could hobble, saying, "Oooh, do you know, Dad, I've come over all queasy. I must go back to bed."

* * *

A quick trip to Madland

Avoid being yourself if you want to attract snoggees. Never EVER be yourself in front of boys. It is not attractive. In each of these incidents I allowed my brain to think for itself. Which is always ALWAYS a mistake. So avoid it. That is what I am saying. Thank you.

Knicker nose sling

Thanks to my mutti and vati's selfish genes (no they are not Levi's) I've inherited the orang-utan gene from Mum and the enormous nose gene from Dad. In fact my dad is practically a nose in trousers. So my whole life is spent trying to keep my nose from spreading all over my face.

Monday October 18th
My room
8:30 p.m.
Mum "suggested" I went to bed early and thought

about the important things in life for once. She's right. I will think about the important things in life. Here goes:

My hair... quite nice in a mousey sort of way. I still think that a blonde streak is a good idea, even after the slight accident I had last time I tried it. The bit that snapped off has grown back now, but I notice Mum has hidden all the toilet cleaners and Grandad's stuff that he puts his false teeth in when he stays. She really is like a police dog.

Anyway, where was I? Oh yes, eyes... Nice, I think, sort of a yellow colour. Jas said I've got cats' eyes.

Nose... Yes well, it doesn't get any smaller. It's the squashiness I don't like. It doesn't seem to have any bone in it. I still can't forget what Grandad said about noses, that as you get older they get bigger and bigger as gravity pulls on them.

8:35 p.m.
You can make a sort of nose sling out of a pair of knickers! Like a sort of anti-gravity device. You put a leg hole over each ear and the middly bit

supports your nose. It's quite comfy. I'm not saying that it looks very glamorous, I'm just saying it's comfy.

8:40 p.m.
It's not something I would wear outside of the privacy of my own bedroom.

8:45 p.m.
It's a good view from my windowsill. I can see Mr Next Door with his stupid poodles. He's all happy now that Angus has gone off poodle baiting in favour of the Burmese sex kitten.

8:46 p.m.
Oh hello, here comes Mark Bog Gob, my ex, the breast fondler. At this rate he will be the one and only fondler. I will die unfondled. He must be coming home from football practice. I don't know how I could ever have thought about snogging him: he wears extremely tragic trousers. He is looking up at my window. He has seen me. He's stopped walking and is looking up at my window.

Staring at me. Well, you know what they say –
once a boy magnet always a boy magnet. I'm just
going to stare back in a really cool way. All right,
Mr Big Gob, Mr Dumper. I might be the dumpee
but you still can't take your eyes away from me,
can you? I still fascinate him. He's just looking up
at me. Just staring and staring. Mesmerised by
me.

8:50 p.m.
Oh my God! I am still wearing my nose hammock
made out of knickers.

8:56 p.m.
Mark will tell all his mates.

8:57 p.m.
He will now call me a knicker-sniffer as well as a
lesbian.

*   *   *

The lurking lurker lurking about lurkily

Tuesday November 2nd
11:00 p.m.

In the car this afternoon Robbie put his head on my knee and sang me one of his songs. It was called, "I'm Not There". I didn't tell Radio Jas that bit.

I never really know what to do with myself when he does his song singing. Maybe nod my head in time to the rhythm?

How attractive is that from upside-down?

And also if you were passing the car as an innocent passer-by you would just see my head bobbling around.

Wednesday November 3rd
7:00 a.m.

In the bathroom I was checking the back of my head and profile. (There's a cabinet which has two mirrors on it. You can look through one and angle the other one so that you can look at the reflection of yourself sideways.) Then I put Mum's magnifying mirror underneath and looked down at myself, because say the Sex God had been lying on my knees sort of looking up at me adoringly and singing (which he had), well I wanted to know what that looked like.

I wish I hadn't bothered for two reasons.

Firstly when I looked down at the mirror I realised that my nose is GIGANTIC. It must have grown overnight. I looked like Gerard Depardieu. Which is not a plus if you are not a forty-eight-year-old French bloke.

Secondly you can definitely see my lurker from underneath.

8:18 a.m.
Jas was waiting for me at her gate.

On the way up the road I said to her, "Do you think my nose is larger than it was yesterday?"

She said, "Don't be silly, noses don't grow."

"Well everything else does – hair, legs, arms... nunga-nungas. Why should your nose be left out?"

She wasn't a bit interested. I went on, "And also can you see I have a lurker up my left nostril?"

She said, "No."

79

"But say you were sort of looking up my nose, from underneath."

She hadn't a clue what I was talking about. She has the imagination of a pea. Half a pea. We were just passing through the park and I tried to explain.

"Well, say I was singing. And you were the Sex God and you were lying with your head in my lap. Looking up adoringly. Marvelling at my enormous talent. Waiting for the appropriate moment to leap on me and snog me to within an inch of my life."

She still didn't get it, so I dragged her over to a bench to illustrate my point. I made her put her head on my lap. I said, "So... what do you think?"

She looked up and said, "I can't hear you singing."

"That's because I'm not."

"But you said what if you were singing?"

Oh for Goodness O'Reilley's trousers' sake!!! To placate her I sang a bit – the only thing that came into my head was "Goldfinger". Singing it brought back horrible memories because Dad and Uncle Eddie had sung it the night Dad came home from

Kiwi-a-gogo. They were both drunk and both wearing leather trousers. Uncle Eddie said, "To impress the ladies." How sad and tragic is that?

Anyway, I was singing "Goldfinger" and Jas had her head on my lap, looking up at my ever-expanding nostrils. Sort of on nostril watch!

I said, "Can you see my lurker up there?"

Then we heard someone behind us having a fit. We leaped up. Well, I did. Jas crashed to the floor. It was Dave the Laugh, absolutely beside himself with laughing. I said, "Er... I was just..."

Jas was going, "I was just looking up... Georgia's nose for... a... bit..."

Dave the L said, "Of course you were. Please don't explain, it will only spoil it for me."

*   *   *

Avoid rubbish luuurve plans

Running about until your head falls off from redness does not make you fit and attractive to boys. It is commonly called a rubbish love plan.

Monday May 2nd
4:30 p.m
Rightio. Part two of my luuuurve plan. Running begins.

4:32 p.m.
It has stopped raining but Gordon Bennet it's nippy noodles, I can see my breath freezing. No chance of nip nip emergence, though, because I have got my nungas safely strapped in.

5:00 p.m.
Phew, I'm boiling and out of breath. I thought I would be quite fit after hockey and everything but I'm not.

5:10 p.m.

I might not be able to breathe but at least I am not being knocked out by my basoomas.

5:15 p.m.

Right, I'm going to just cut across the top of the field and then come down the hill and come home.

Can heads explode? Because I think mine is going to.

5:16 p.m.

There is some other fool out running. I can hear pounding along behind me but I haven't got the strength to look round. When I get home I am going to get in the fridge, I am so hot and red.

"*Ciao*, Georgia."

Ohmygiddygodspyjamas, Masimo!!!

Noooooooooooooooooooooo.

He caught up with me and was running alongside me. I just kept running and turned and gave him what I hoped was an attractive smile. Attractive if you like a smiling tomato in a jogging outfit. He looked sooo cool, and not even sweating. Also he seemed to be able to breathe. And talk.

He said, "You know, I didn't get your phone number. Would it be possible that you tell me?"

I gave him another smile. It might be the last living thing I did. Then I saw the hill path and my brain was so starved of oxygen it had no control over any part of my body. My legs started stumbling down the hill path. They were just merrily careering down the path, carrying my head and body along with them. Thank God Masimo didn't follow me. As he continued along the top path he shouted, "OK, Miss Hard to Get, I will see you later when I get back from America, *ciao caro*."

At that point the hill path curved around and I crashed into a bush and fell over.

In bed
9:30 p.m.
Oh ow ow. Ouch and ow.

He wanted my telephone number and I couldn't speak. I could only be very very red.

I can't stand this.

*   *   *

Snogtastic hints

Now then, if you are at all not bonkers, you might be thinking, erm, is it really worth doing snogging and having the Horn? As quite frankly it seems to make some people (me) look like a fool and a ponce and lead to heartbreakosity and merde. Well, for goodness sake, what is the point of me going through all this for you (and I do it, as I have said before, only because I really really love you) if you are not going to go out there and snog for England?

Yes, the snog fest can be fraught with danger and poo, you may meet a Whelk Boy or a Mark Big Gob, and sometimes your boy entrancers will fall off. But on the other hand, there may be a Luuurve God lurking round the corner, or a Sex God, or a Dave the Laugh. So come on, gird your loins and follow my advice to become a successful sex kitty...

How to make any twit fall in love with you

I found this book in my mutti's drawer. It is full of

marvy boy-entrancing tips. The main thing to remember is that boys are simple creatures and knob centred. (Well, that's what Dave the Laugh says. Mind you he did also say that he wanted to be a girl so he could spend all day looking at his nunga-nungas.)

Thursday March 10th
7:45 p.m.
What is this book that Mutti has hidden in her knickers drawer?

How to Make Anyone Fall in Love with You.

8:00 p.m.
This is amazing.

8:30 p.m.
Phoned Rosie.

"Rosie."

"*Quoi?*"

"Do you know how to make anyone fall in love with you?"

"Well, in Sven's case I reel him in with snacks and snogging."

I've seen the two of them snogging and eating snacks at the same time, so I didn't really want to talk about it much.

I went on, "My mutti has got a secret book and it tells you how to make anyone fall in love with you, even normal boys, boys who are not Svens."

Friday March 11th
8:00 p.m.
Ellen, Jools, Rosie, Mabs, Jas and me were trying out different make-up techniques and hairstyles. I showed them Mutti's book, which I have sneaked into my room.

They all sat down on my bed and I started to read stuff out. They were ogling me like goosegogs.

I said, "OK, this is really cool, it tells you how to become a boy magnet *extraordinaire*. There is a list. Number one is, let me see, oh yes... 'Smile broadly'."

We practised smiling broadly. Good grief, how scary Jas is when she smiles broadly. Surely boys don't like this? Perhaps I read it wrong. Nope, it definitely says that boys like you to smile broadly. Still, there are limits.

I said to Jas, "Jas, if you don't mind me saying, your broad smile is a bit scary potatoes."

She went all huffy and red. "Well, you've got some room to talk, Georgia. When you smile broadly your nose is about four feet wide."

Oh charming. That is the thanks you get for trying to be a good pal.

Ellen said, "OK, my face is aching a bit from the smiling thing. What is the next tip?"

I looked at the book. "'Throw him darting glances'."

We practised throwing each other darting glances. Easy peasy.

Number three was dance alone to the music. I put on a CD and we practised dancing alone to it. Do you know my new taut and all-encompassing nunga-nunga holders really do keep my nungas under control. Even if I leap wildly in the air and jiggle my shoulders around to the music.

I shouted to Jas above the music, "Is there any evidence of nip nip emergence in this top?"

She began peering at my nungas really close up. I said, "Stop it, lezzie, I only asked you to glance for nip nip emergence. I didn't ask you to ogle my nungas."

She really got the megahump then and tried *ignorez-vous*ing me. She didn't storm off in a strop, though, because she wanted to know what number four on the list was. I said, "Okeydokey, number four is... 'Look straight at him and flip your hair'."

We did excellent hair flipping. Which is what we mostly do all day anyway.

Number five was "Look at him, look away, toss your head and then look back."

There was a lot of tossing and so on until I got a really bad neck cramp.

Number six was quite hilarious. "Lick your lips and parade close to him with exaggerated hip movements."

Rosie started doing it round the room. I said, "Surely boys don't like this. You look like you've got replacement hips."

The next one was a bit more sensible. It said you

had to do "sticky eyes". You have to sort of look him in the eyes and then drag your eyes away from his as if they've been stuck with warm toffee.

In my house it is quite likely that you could wake up with toffee in your eyes, but I don't suppose that is what the author has in mind.

The girls all crashed off home with plenty of things to think about and practise for tomorrow. I watched them out my window doing the hip thing down the street like elderly hula dancers in overcoats.

I felt a bit cheered up.

Midnight
Only nineteen hours till Rosie's teenage werewolf party.

12:05 a.m.
What do I care though? I have given up boys.

Saturday March 12th
Rosie's house
9:00 p.m.
Quite a crowd at the party. All the usual suspects.

Sam and his mates from sixth form college, the Foxwood crowd, Damion Knightly (known as the Dame) and his mates from St John's plus loads of girls we knew from gigs and Moorgrange School. Some of the boys were quite fit, but none had that *je ne sais quoi*, that Sex Goddy charm that brought out the red-bottomosity in me.

And no sign of Dave the Laugh.

Good. At least I could relax.

Jas said, "Dave the Laugh's not here."

I said, "So?"

And she just looked at me. She is turning quite literally into a staring person.

9:15 p.m.

I thought just for a laugh I would try out some of the tactics from Mutti's book.

The Dame came over and said, "Hi, Gee, come and dance about like a prat." And he pulled me on to the dance floor (the bit in between the sofa and the dining table). The Dame was blundering around to some really loud rock music that Sven had put on. Sven was actually on the table thrusting his furry shorts around like a sort of Viking lap dancer.

Rosie was doing the twist very very fast till she was a blur of fur.

Anyway, I thought for practice I would try "sticky eyes" on the Dame. So I looked him in the eyes. He looked a bit startled at first, like he was thinking, "Oy what are you looking at, mate?" But I did that dragging my eyes away from his thing and then looking back. And it worked!!! He was sort of mesmerised. In fact it was a bit like I had hypnotised him. I kept looking him in the eye and then I moved to the fireplace, still looking at him. And he followed me there like a boy zombie. I went behind the TV and he followed me there. I went and stood by the window and he followed me there. It was amazing.

Then Dave the Laugh walked in. Gadzooks and also crikey! He was dressed all in black like me and he looked cool. His hair was slicked back and he had false fangs. Which I am alarmed to say I found a bit attractive. You could do excellent lip nibbling with them.

I had stopped looking at the Dame but he still followed me as I went to the snacks and drinks table. I was sort of casually pretending that I hadn't even noticed Dave the Laugh. Which was a bit difficult to keep up, because he shouted, "OK all you chicks who find me irresistible, follow me. No pushing."

Oh vair vair *amusant*. He's so bloody confident. He went off into the kitchen and a few girls (including Ellen, who as we know has no pride to speak of) went after him. I was just looking at the kitchen door when Dave suddenly appeared back through it again. I was so shocked that I turned round really quickly and practically snogged the Dame, who was lurking behind me.

He said, looking all dreamy and hypnotised, "Do you fancy going outside?"

I said, "Er, it's minus a million degrees out there."

And he said, "I'll keep you warm."

Is there a crap book that useless boys read called *Tips for Being Useless*? If there is, the Dame has read it. I didn't even bother replying. Then

Ellen came dithering over to me. She was all red and spazzy.

"He's – you know, well, he's... I... should I... well, you know?"

I said, "Ellen, look, don't have a nervy b. It's not attractive. Listen, why don't you try that dancing-on-your-own tactic?"

She thought that was a good idea and started dancing around looking all dreamy and moody, and slightly swishing her hair about. Within seconds one of Sam's mates started dancing with her.

Surely this how-to-make-anyone-fall-in-love-with-you thing can't be this easy?

Dave the Laugh was looking at me, but I wasn't going for it, fangs or no fangs. I could go up to him and say, "Hi, Dave. 'Bye, Dave. You are so yesterday, but fangs for the memory."

Shut up, brain!!!

He was looking at me but he didn't come over, so I thought I would go look at the CD collection in a sort of cool way because the tension was making me want to go to the piddly-diddly department.

I had to walk past him to get to the CDs so I flicked my hair a bit and did the hip-waggling thing. (Which is not as easy to coordinate as you might think.)

Yess!!! Result is he followed me. I was looking at the CDs even though I realised at the last minute that they were all upside down and I couldn't see the titles. He said, "Georgia."

I didn't even turn round.

"Georgia, I know your hips are bad but do you fancy a quick snog? I've got healing hands."

He is appalling!!!

It sort of made me laugh, though. He is soooo full of himself.

I turned round to him and looked at him like it said in the book (the bit I hadn't told the Ace Gang yet). It said, "Number eight. Let your eyes slide down the nose to the lips, caress the lips with your eyes for a moment and then slowly venture south to the neck."

Dave took his fangs out and said, "So, Sex Kitty... "

*　　*　　*

How to practise snogging with the aid of your mate's leg and a false beard

Saturday 11th June
2:00 p.m.

All the gang gathered at Rosie's for my practice date.

Rosie said she would be Masimo, and the rest of them would watch and be the judges, like in a sort of snogging *Come Dancing*.

Come Snogging, in fact.

2:10 p.m.

Rosie went off to her bedroom. She said, "I'm going to be Masimo, so I have to get in the mood for luuurve."

She came back five minutes later wearing a false beard, with a banana down her jeans.

I said, "Why have you got a banana down your jeans?"

Rosie said, "It was Sven's suggestion. He said it is representative of the pant python."

Ellen said, "I, er... do you mean like a boy's, er, well..."

Rosie said, "Exactomondo, my little pally." Which was a bit off-putting, actually.

Jas said, "OK, let's get on, because I have to get home earlyish. It's only ninety-nine hours till Tom gets home and I must prepare myself. What will you do when you first see him?" She pointed to Rosie, who was walking in a very peculiar way and waggling her beard. "There he is tall, tanned, Italian, sophisticated. So what do you do?"

I said, "Er, leap on him and snog him within an inch of his life? Taking care not to strangle myself on his false beard, or disturb his banana."

Jools said, "What does it say in the *How to Make Any Twit Fall in Love with You* book?"

Mabs was officially in charge of the book, so she looked up "first impressions".

3:00 p.m.
I have to hip wiggle up to him, look at him, look away, fiddle with my hair and do a bit of flicking. If I have any spare time I need to lick my lips a bit.

Mabs said, "The book says you should say

something light and interesting to start the conversation. Also, if he says anything funny, you have to laugh like the proverbial drain."

I did hip wiggle, flicky, licky over to Rosie, while the rest of them sat looking and chewing. Rosie said (in what she imagines is an Italian accent but actually sounds like a fool), "*Ciao.*"

I said, "*Ciao.* Er, *prego.*"

"*Ciao.*"

All the gang were ogling me.

I said, "Masimo, did you know that the Spartans... you know in the old days of Sparta, which is quite nearish to Italy..."

Rosie had pretended to fall asleep. She said, "Get on with it."

I said, "Well, they used to keep teenage boys half-starved so that they had to go out and steal food, and if they got caught they would beat them to within an inch of their lives."

They all just looked at me.

Mabs said, "Do you call that light and interesting?"

I do actually. That is the deep sadnosity of my

life; I find it vair difficult to be as superficial as others.

An hour later
I am allowed to mention music, the weather, or something to do with him.

I said, "Yeah, but all I know about him is that I fancy the arse off him."

5:00 p.m.
After four packets of reviving Pringles we have managed to decide on, "*Ciao*, great to see you." and "What a fine evening." Providing it is not tipping it down, which would make me a fool.

Now on to the meal.

Essentially, I have to pretend to eat a lot, but not really eat anything in case I choke to death.

Jas said, "You could have a nourishing soup, but don't do that slurping thing that you do."

I said, "What slurping thing?"

Jas said, "Oh, I can't go in to it now, I have to be

off. I'm just saying don't do it." And she went off.

How annoying is she?

6:00 p.m.

I have to listen to him a LOT.

Jools said, "And when you laugh, don't do your ad hoc laughing and let your nose spread all over your face."

6:30 p.m.

Then we got on to the snogging bit.

I said, "Do you think Italians snog the same as English boys?"

Rosie said, "I don't know if they do anything different with their tongues or what their ear work is like. You will have to give us a complete and full report. What number will you let him go up to on the first date?"

"I thought number four. A kiss lasting over three minutes without a break suggests deep sensuality without going that little bit too far into acting like a tart."

Then Rosie said, "Finally, as you haven't had

any snogging practice for a while, try an experimental snog on the back of my leg."

What??? Absolutely not, not a snowball's chance in hell.

No and three times NO.

6:45 p.m.

On my knees snogging the back of Rosie's leg while the Ace Gang watch me.

Why am I doing this?

Rosie was shouting instructions. "Yes, yes, that's good. Good. And breathe. Too much teeth!! Too much teeth!!! A bit more sucky. Flicky tongue and... finish."

Good grief. Have you ever snogged the back of someone's leg? Someone who is one of your mates and is wearing a false beard? Well, I hope you never have to, that is all I'm saying.

7:00 p.m.

I said as I was leaving, "Do you think I should ask him what his intentions are vis à vis Old Thongy?"

Mabs said, "I think you should act as if she

doesn't exist and just find a way to subtly undermine her."

Hmmm. Good advice.

We are indeed the Wise Women of the Forest of Snog.

* * *

Final Words of Wisdomosity

That's it, little chumettes! A brief (but clearly the work of a genius) guide to snogging. So sound your Cosmic Horns! And remember the snoggers' song, "Snog on, snog on, with hope in your heart and you'll never snog alone! You'll never snog alone!!!"

Thank you and goodnight. Do you know I am absolutely full of exhaustiosity. I will probably never be able to sleep or snog again. I feel that I have given my all (oo-er) and that I have worn myself to a frazzle on your behalf. I've got that exhaustiosity where you are vair vair tired but you still can't go to slee...

...zzzzzzzzzzzzzzzzzzzzzzzzz.

Georgia's Glossary

boy entrancers · False eyelashes. Boys are ALWAYS entranced when you wear them. This is a FACT… unless of course they get stuck together and then boys think you are mad and blind and not entrancing at all.

bum-oley · Quite literally bottom hole. I'm sorry, but you did ask. Say it proudly (with a cheery smile and a Spanish accent).

Kiwi-a-gogo land · New Zealand. "a-gogo land" can be used to liven up the otherwise really boring names of other countries. America, for instance, is Hamburger-a-gogo land. Mexico is Mariachi-a-gogo land and France is Frogs'-legs-a-gogo land.

Hoooorn · The Particular Horn is when you fancy the arse off one boy. The General Horn is when you fancy all boys. And the Cosmic Horn is when you fancy everybody and everything in the universe – even doorknobs.

nervy spaz · Nervous spasm. Nearly the same as a nervy b. (nervous breakdown) or an F.T. (funny turn), only more spectacular on the physical side.

nippy noodles · Instead of saying, "Good heavens, it's quite cold this morning!" you say, "Cor – nippy noodles!!" English is an exciting and growing language. It is. Believe me. Just leave it at that. Accept it.

nuddy-pants · Quite literally nude-coloured pants. And you know what nude-coloured pants are? They are no pants. So if you are in your nuddy-pants you are in your no pants (i.e. you are naked).

nunga-nungas · Basoomas. Girl's breasty business. Dave the Laugh calls them nunga-nungas because he says that if you get hold of a girl's breast and pull it out and then let it go, it goes nunga-nunga-nunga. As I have said many, many times with great wisdomosity, there is something really wrong with boys.

red-bottomosity · Having the big red bottom. This is vair vair interesting *vis à vis* nature. When a lady baboon is "in the mood" for luuurve, she displays her big red bottom to the male baboon. (Apparently he wouldn't have a clue otherwise, but that is boys for you!) Anyway, if you hear the call of the Horn, you are said to be displaying red-bottomosity.

Whelk Boy · A whelk is a horrible shellfish thing that only the truly mad eat. Slimy and mucus-like. Whelk boy is a boy who kisses like a whelk, i.e. a slimy mucus kisser. Erlack a pongoes.

The Snogging Scale

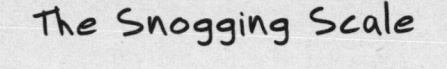

½. sticky eyes (*Be careful using this. I've still got some complete twit following me around like a seeing-eye dog.*)

1. holding hands

2. arm around

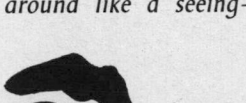

3. goodnight kiss

4. kiss lasting over three minutes without a breath (*What you need for this is a sad mate who's got a watch and no boyfriend.*)

5. open mouth kissing

6. tongues

6½. ear snogging

6¾. neck nuzzling

7. upper body fondling - outdoors

8. upper body fondling - indoors (in bed)

9. below waist activity (or bwa)

10. the full monty (*Jas and I were in the room when Dad was watching the news and the newscaster said, "Tonight the Prime Minister has reached Number 10." And Jas and I had a laughing spaz to end all laughing spazzes.*)